# Dear Parent:
## Your child's love of reading starts here!

Every child learns to read in a different way and at his or her own speed. Some go back and forth between reading levels and read favorite books again and again. Others read through each level in order. You can help your young reader improve and become more confident by encouraging his or her own interests and abilities. From books your child reads with you to the first books he or she reads alone, there are I Can Read Books for every stage of reading:

### SHARED READING
Basic language, word repetition, and whimsical illustrations, ideal for sharing with your emergent reader

### BEGINNING READING
Short sentences, familiar words, and simple concepts for children eager to read on their own

### READING WITH HELP
Engaging stories, longer sentences, and language play for developing readers

### READING ALONE
Complex plots, challenging vocabulary, and high-interest topics for the independent reader

### ADVANCED READING
Short paragraphs, chapters, and exciting themes for the perfect bridge to chapter books

**I Can Read Books** have introduced children to the joy of reading since 1957. Featuring award-winning authors and illustrators and a fabulous cast of beloved characters, I Can Read Books set the standard for beginning readers.

A lifetime of discovery begins with the magical words **"I Can Read!"**

*Visit www.icanread.com for information*
*on enriching your child's reading experience.*

# JUST A
# LITTLE SICK

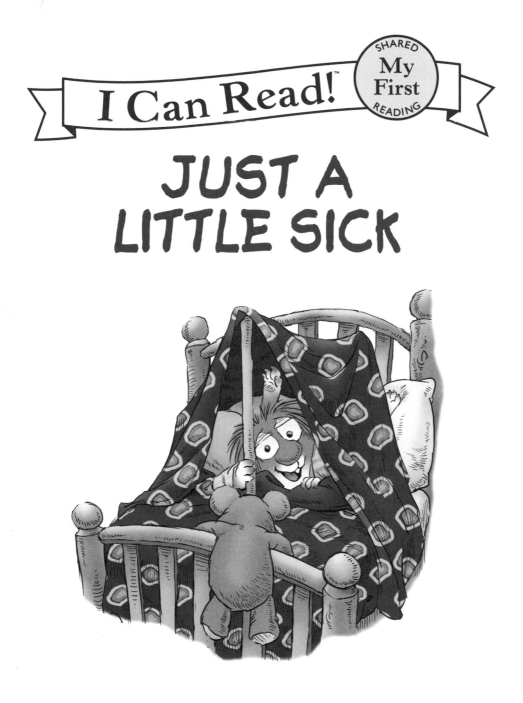

# BY MERCER MAYER

**HARPER**

*An Imprint of HarperCollinsPublishers*

*To Diane, Bonnie, and Rita,*
*the elves*

I Can Read Book® is a trademark of HarperCollins Publishers.

Library of Congress catalog card number: 2009922327

ISBN 978-0-06-083556-9 (trade bdg.) —ISBN 978-0-06-083555-2 (pbk.)

Typography by Diane Dubreuil

15  16  17  18   PC/WOR    10 9 8 7 6 5

❖

First Edition

 A Big Tuna Trading Company, LLC/J. R. Sansevere Book
www.littlecritter.com

I am just a little sick today.
Mom says, "No school.
You need to stay in bed."

Being just a little sick
is fun.

I get breakfast in bed. Yay!

It is just plain toast. Yuck!

"I want Fruity Nut Crunch,"
I say.

Mom says, "You are too sick.
Go back to bed."

"I am not too sick
to play video games."

"Yes, you are," says Mom.
"Now go to bed and rest."

I am not too sick
to fly to the moon
on my rocket ship.

"The rocket ship ran out
of gas," Mom says.
"It needs to rest."

15

I am not too sick
to build a tent on my bed.
I am hiding from my bear.

Suddenly I don't feel good.

My bear and I go to find Mom.

Mom sends me back to bed.
She takes my temperature.

"You have a fever," says Mom.

I say, "I am sleepy."

I wake up from my nap.
I feel great!

I get dressed.

I will go out to play.

Mom says, "Oh, good,
you are all dressed.
Let's go to the doctor."

"But I am not sick anymore,"
I say.

Mom takes me to the doctor
anyway.

We wait and wait.

I put on a funny-looking robe.
The back is open.

The doctor checks my throat,
my nose, and my ears.

The doctor gives Mom something
to make me feel better.

We go home.
I can't wait to go out
and play with my friends.

"Oh, no," says Mom.
"The doctor said
you have to rest all day."

I am tired of resting!
I ask, "Can I please go
to school tomorrow?"

I changed my mind.
Being just a little sick
is no fun.